ARTHUR'S SWORD

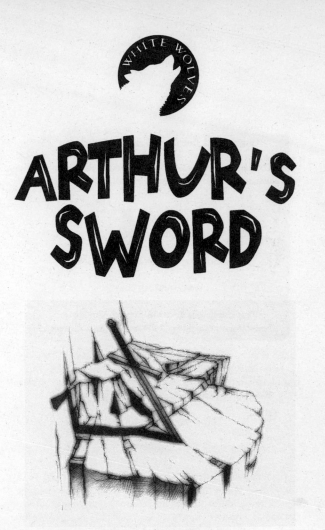

ARTHUR'S SWORD

Sophie McKenzie
Illustrated by Gianluca Garofalo

A & C Black • London

White Wolves Series Consultant: Sue Ellis,

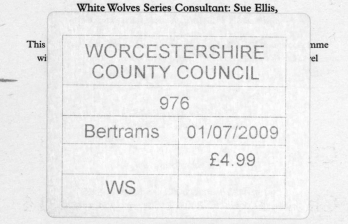
The rights of Sohpie McKenzie and Gianluca Garofalo
to be identified as author and illustrator of this work
respectively have been asserted by them in accordance with
the Copyrights, Designs and Patents Act 1988.

ISBN 978-0-7136-8815-3

A CIP catalogue for this book is available from the British Library.

This book is produced using paper that is made from wood
grown in managed, sustainable forests. It is natural, renewable and
recyclable. The logging and manufacturing processes conform
to the environmental regulations of the country of origin.

Printed and bound in Great Britain
by CPI Cox & Wyman, Reading RG1 8EX.

CONTENTS

CHAPTER ONE

Thud. Thwack. Arthur hit Kay's
sword again.

The wooden sword
flew out of Kay's
hands. It
clattered
to the
courtyard
floor.

Arthur grinned. He was beating his foster brother, even though Kay was older and bigger and stronger than him.

"You cheated," Kay said.

"No, I didn't."

Arthur and Kay practised sword-fighting every day. It was part of Kay's training to become a knight.

Arthur stood back to give Kay time to pick up his sword. The sun shone. It glinted off the stained-glass window in the nearby chapel.

Wham.

Kay swung his sword and knocked Arthur off his feet.

"Aargh!" Arthur landed with a bump on his bottom. "Ow!"

"Serves you right." Kay towered over Arthur, his eyes glaring. "How *dare* you hit my sword away."

"I beat you fair and square," said Arthur. He scrambled up and backed towards the chapel.

Kay swung his sword again. Arthur ducked.

Smash. Kay's sword hit the chapel window. Coloured glass shattered onto the ground.

Arthur stared in horror. Glass was precious. His foster father, Sir Ector, would be furious when he saw what Kay had done.

"That was your fault," said Kay.

"No, it wasn't."

Arthur looked round. No one was in the courtyard. No one had heard the glass smash.

"Yes, it was," said Kay. "You broke that window. I saw you."

Arthur's heart sank. Sir Ector was a good man, but he always believed Kay.

"That's not fair," Arthur yelled.

He turned and ran out of the courtyard. He was so angry that he kept running, right into the forest.

Why was Kay so mean? Was it because Arthur wasn't his real brother?

Arthur wished he knew who his real parents were.

He stopped by a tree.

"By King Uther!" said a deep voice.

Arthur jumped. There, in front of him, was the strangest-looking man he had ever seen.

CHAPTER TWO

The man was tall, with a long, white beard. His eyes were bright blue, the same colour as his robes.

"What are *you* doing here?"
the man exclaimed.

"I'm Sir Ector's foster-son.
He owns this forest," said Arthur.
"What are *you* doing here?"

"I'm Merlin," the man said. "I live here."

Arthur looked round. He couldn't see a house.

The man laughed. "It's a pleasure to meet you *again*, Arthur."

Arthur frowned. "How do you know my name? And what do you mean, 'meet you again'? Have you met me before?"

"That's a lot of questions," Merlin said. "I'm not good with questions before breakfast."

Arthur frowned. "But it's nearly lunchtime."

"By King Uther, then we
must eat!" Merlin stood back.
A rug lay on the ground, covered
with delicious food.

Arthur was sure it hadn't been there before. But he didn't like to ask more questions. And he was hungry. So he sat down and ate.

"Do you like living at the castle?" said Merlin.

"Actually, I've run away," Arthur said. "It's Kay. He hates me because I'm better at sword-fighting than him. He's older, you see, and will be a knight. I'll only be his squire. That's like a helper. I wish *I* could be a knight."

"Ah." Merlin threw a sweetmeat into the air and caught it in his mouth. "Do you think a knight would run away from home?"

Arthur thought about this. "I suppose not," he said.

"Ah," Merlin said again. "What would a knight do?"

Arthur sighed. "Be brave and go back to the castle."

So Arthur and Merlin walked back to the castle together. As they arrived, Sir Ector and Kay appeared.

"Arthur!" Sir Ector's roar echoed round the courtyard. He pointed to the chapel. "Kay says you broke..."

Sir Ector's mouth fell open.

Arthur looked. He couldn't believe his eyes. The glass in the window was mended.

"What does this mean?"
Sir Ector said.

"It means that a squire needs as much help as a knight." Merlin winked at Arthur. "And that I would like to help train Arthur to be Kay's squire."

Chapter Three

Several years passed. Kay became a knight and Arthur his squire.

One day, Arthur was polishing
Kay's armour when a messenger
rode up to the castle.

"Hail, Sir Ector," he said.
"I bring sad news. King Uther
is dead and leaves no heir.
A tournament is being held to
decide who will replace him.

All the knights in the land will compete."

Arthur was sad about Uther, but excited, too. He had never been to a tournament before.

A week later, Arthur, Sir Ector, Sir Kay, and Merlin arrived at the tournament.

Arthur couldn't believe how many knights there were, sword-fighting and jousting and competing in archery contests.

Everywhere he looked, there was noise and colour.

A crowd had gathered around
a large rock.

"What's everyone looking at?"
Kay said.

Arthur strained his eyes.
Something silver was poking out
of the rock.

"It's a sword," he said.

Sir Ector frowned. "What's
a sword doing in the middle of
a rock?"

"Ah," said Merlin.

Arthur went closer. He pushed his way through the crowd. Some words were carved in the stone.

"*Whoever pulls the sword from this stone shall be king of all England.*"

"Well, that's easy." Kay stepped forward, grabbed the sword and pulled. The sword didn't move. Kay tugged harder. Nothing.

Red-faced, Kay stepped back.

"Don't worry, son," said one of the knights standing nearby. "We've all tried. It's impossible."

Arthur stared at the sword. He wanted to try, too.

"Perhaps I...?" Sir Ector strode over to the sword. He struggled for a few minutes, then gave up.

Arthur didn't know why, but he was sure he could pull the sword from the stone.

"Look at Arthur," Kay laughed. "He wants a go."

The other knights laughed. Arthur blushed.

"He has as much right to try as anyone else," Merlin said.

"Go on then, boy," Sir Ector smiled.

Arthur stepped forwards.

He gripped the sword tightly.

He pulled.

In one smooth move, the sword came free.

CHAPTER FOUR

The knights' laughter died away.

Arthur looked at the steel sword. It was almost as long as he was, but it felt light in his hands.

"Well, well," Merlin said. "It seems we have found the new king of England."

Excited chatter filled the air. Arthur gasped. King of England? It couldn't be possible.

"No way!" Kay's voice broke through the noise. "Arthur's only a boy. He isn't even a noble."

The knights fell silent. Arthur looked round. Everyone seemed to be waiting for him to say something, but he had no idea what.

"Actually," Merlin said.
"Arthur is King Uther's son
and his true heir."

Arthur almost dropped
the sword. King Uther's son?
He looked up. Merlin's
blue eyes twinkled.

"What?" Kay shouted. "Who says?"

"Yes," said one of the other knights. "How do you know?"

"Because when he was born," said Merlin, "I promised King Uther to find a home for him until this day came."

"By Uther, who'd have thought?" Sir Ector dropped to his knees. "Well done, my boy. I mean... sire."

Arthur looked in amazement as several of the other knights knelt, too.

"Stop!" Kay shouted. "This is ridiculous. Arthur can't be king. Just because he pulled that stupid sword out of the rock..."

Arthur tugged at Merlin's long, blue robe. "What should I do?" he whispered.

"You'll work it out," Merlin winked.

"Well?" Kay snapped.

Arthur needed time to think.

"We should go inside," he said.
He marched towards the castle.
All the knights followed. Then
everyone else at the tournament
followed them.

As they reached the castle
doors, Arthur's heart pounded.
He still had no idea what to do.

Inside the castle, his footsteps
echoed on the stone floor. The
Great Hall was empty.

Then Arthur noticed the fireplace. It was full of sticks, ready for the evening fire.

Of course.

Arthur smiled. Merlin was right, he *was* the true king. And he had just worked out how to make everyone else believe it.

CHAPTER FIVE

Arthur reached into the fireplace and took out a stick. He faced the huge crowd.

"This stick is England," he said.

"Looks like a bit of wood to me," Kay said.

The knights sniggered.

"This stick is England under King Uther," Arthur went on. "Strong and unbroken."

Kay snorted. He grabbed the stick and snapped it in two. "And here's England under King Arthur – in pieces."

The other knights laughed.

Kay broke each stick again. Now there were four pieces.

"And this is England today." Arthur gathered up the pieces. "With everybody arguing."

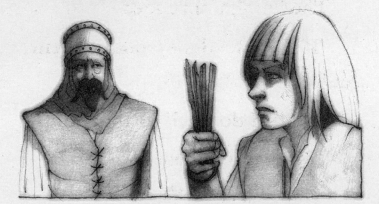

"So what magic are you going to use to put England back together, boy?" Sir Ector chuckled.

Arthur glanced at Merlin.

Merlin smiled. "Go on, Arthur."

Arthur took a deep breath. "I can show you how to stop these sticks from breaking." He looked round at the knights. "If I do, will you accept me as your king?"

The knights shrugged.

"It can't be done," one of them said.

"But if I do it...?" Arthur said.

"Oh, yes, my liege," Kay said sarcastically. "Do show us the amazing secret of the unbreakable sticks."

"OK." Arthur undid his belt. He wound it round the four pieces of stick and tied it tight. Then he handed the bundle to Kay. "Now try."

Kay took the bunch of sticks and tried to break it. But the sticks were too strong.

Frowning, Kay passed the bundle to Sir Ector. He couldn't break it, either. Then every knight in the room tried, and failed, to snap the bunch of sticks.

"These sticks are the knights of

England," Arthur said. "Separate, we are weak and easily broken. Together, we are strong."

"Well done, my boy," said Sir Ector. He dropped to his knees. "Hail, Arthur, king of England."

One by one, all the knights knelt before Arthur.

"I'm sorry, Arthur." Kay was last to kneel. "You are indeed a worthy king."

Everyone cheered.

Arthur raised his sword. He smiled – relieved and excited all at once. And, with Merlin at his side, he led everyone outside, into the sunshine.

About the Author

Sophie McKenzie was born and brought up in London, where she still lives. She has written a number of books including the award-winning *Girl, Missing* and the thriller *Blood Ties*.

She has always loved the story of Arthur because it involves magic, big emotions, lots of conflict, love, power, self-belief and an ordinary person realising that he can achieve extraordinary things. In other words – all the best ingredients for storytelling!

Year 3

Stories with Familiar Settings

Detective Dan • Vivian French

Buffalo Bert • Michaela Morgan

Treasure at the Boot-fair • Chris Powling

Mystery and Adventure Stories

Scratch and Sniff • Margaret Ryan

The Thing in the Basement • Michaela Morgan

On the Ghost Trail • Chris Powling

Myths and Legends

Pandora's Box • Rose Impey

Sephy's Story • Julia Green

Wings of Icarus • Jenny Oldfield

Arthur's Sword • Sophie McKenzie

Hercules the Hero • Tony Bradman

Beowulf the Brave • Julia Green